MY JOURNEY

TO THE WELL

I0524874

Keyshia Anderson

Publication Information

The Well Publishing Company

Library of Congress Control Number: In publication data

ISBN# 978-0-9991590-6-4

My Journey to the Well

Author: Keyshia Anderson

Cover Design: The Liar's Craft

Interior Design: LaShele Jones-Evans

Publisher: The Well Publishing Company

PUBLISHER'S NOTE:

Table of Contents

ACKNOWLEDGEMENTS

I would like to thank the Lord for my husband, Richard Anderson. Ten and a half years of being together, three and a half years of marriage, and twenty-one years of memories of our first encounter. The evidence of yet another "Great Encounter." It had to be God that it lingered for eleven years and was still able to manifest. I am ever so grateful that we allowed Him to do it and on His time. I know if we had of tried to do it back then we would have messed it up. He had to take us through some things to prepare us for each other. I thank and praise God for my journey. If it had not been for my journey, I would not have been able to endure the bad times that came along in the midst of the good ones. Yes, we've had quite a few bad times, but if there were no bad ones, we would not have been able to appreciate all the good ones. And it is because of you that I have not had to do it alone, all over again. I thank you for being there with me and our boys – Na'Kahi, Richard and Elijah. The completion of my six pack. I am not exactly sure what was in the water, however God knew I did not have it in me to do it by myself again. The bible says the Lord would not put more on us than we can bear. But with their energy level the way it is, it would have been tragic.

To Tykeyshia, Robert and Jhahid. My first loves! I think that song just about sums it all up. There was another popular song out during this time. Babies having Babies. This is exactly what I was. A baby having babies. My first one three months before my 16th birthday, the next one two months after turning 18 and the last one five months before I turned 20. This thing did not come with an owner's manual. But knowing what I know now, I would be able to write one to share the experience with those who like me are "Babies having Babies", with no one to show them how to parent. A good friend of mine says all the time, how she was a good parent but not good at parenting! We would be able to make money with that one.

To a very special woman. A great preacher, teacher, evangelist and prophetess. She spoke life into my lifeless self. She gave me hope when I was hopeless. She showed me the way to live. A true Women of God indeed, with such a sweet spirit. A woman of God whom I was able to sit at her feet and learn. The day you transitioned, a shift took place in my life. In the beginning I was unable to comprehend the shift. God began to deal with me in some ways that I did not understand. It was not fair. I was not ready. However, I realized, you helped prepare me for what was to come. It was not until I came to grips with my "Disconnect Notice", then I was able to stand up and face my journey to the well, to become a WELL Woman. To Lady Betty Ann Graham, may you sleep in peace!

To my first real pastor - The Honorable Doctor Apostle John T. Graham. The Lord gave you the strength and the patience to pastor me for 19 years. You have seen me through the good and through the bad. You have to have a special calling on your life to be able to serve God in the capacity of a Pastor and deal with a church full of folk like me. Me alone I'm sure kept you praying. But you did not give up on me. You showed love and compassion. Through all of your preaching and teaching, you have helped me grow into the Woman of God I am today. Temple United Church will always be my home. THE LITTLE CHURCH IN THE MIDDLE OF THE BLOCK, WITH A BIG HEART FOR ALL THE PEOPLE! And to Lady Matrue Graham. I love you and I truly thank you! I thank you for being you and helping me P.U.S.H. (Pray Until Something Happened). You pushed me to pray and seek the face of the Lord. I questioned a lot of things. I still do not have all of the answers, but apparently it is not for me to know. As long as God knows, that is all that matters. I will settle for knowing that all things work together for the good that love the Lord and are the called according to His purpose and that He would not put no more on us than we could bare.

To Pastor Lashele Jones-Evans. I have followed you for quite a few years. You have literally lifted my spirit on so many occasions, long before you ever knew it. You have such a sweet spirit. It reminds me of my spiritual mother, Betty Ann Graham (S.I.P.). You truly have a gift and a special anointing and you share it so freely. I cannot thank you enough, for you as a person and your ministries. Continue to L.I.F.T., the name of Jesus first and others second. The motivation and encouragement that you exhibit and the drive you put into other people's success, you have no choice but to be successful.

To Author K.D. Harris. WOW, is all I can say. I thank you for the confidence and the encouragement you gave me throughout this project. I thank you for listening and being obedient to even start the project. I knew in my mind that I had a book in me since around 1999. Although this is not that book, it is a step towards that book. I thank you pushing me and working with me. I thank you for your patience (I pray you still have some left); as I am sure many a times I got on your very last nerve. But I cannot thank you enough for helping me see this through!!!

DEDICATIONS

To the Well Woman Empowerment Association and to all of the WELL Woman around the world…This book I dedicate to you!

Introduction

I cannot say that I have been in church all my life, like some can. But for the 19 years that I have been in church, I've heard enough sermons to assist me in this journey called life. I've heard about Adam and Eve and how important it is to listen and obey the instructions of the Lord and not allow the enemy to use the word to trip you up. I heard about Abraham being told to separate from his family. I remember hearing about Moses and the burning bush and how the Lord allowed him to lead the people across the Red Sea. But also how an 11 day journey, took 40 years because of their murmuring and complaining. I'm sure I am not the only one that can tell you about David; Job; The Prophets - Isaiah, Jeremiah, Ezekiel; Daniel and Jonah.

I am also certain when you get to the Gospels – Matthew, Mark, Luke and John – there are certain stories that get preached about more than others. The birth of Jesus and three wise men;

John the Baptist and the Sermon on the Mount. We hear about how all the miracles Jesus performed, how he choose the 12 disciples and the ever so popular Woman at the Well. When you hear the story of the woman at the well, you generally hear about her not so Christian lifestyle, how she had 5 husbands and the one she is with now, is not hers. You hear of how she came to the well in the middle of the day to avoid having to make contact with others, particularly the other women in the community.

After years of hearing the sermons being preached the same and listening to others relay their version of her story. I was given a version of my own to relay. Instead of the promiscuous, "Lady of the Night", that has been said to have been around town, per se, I see a young lady who has had to deal with a lot of issues. Real life issues that some were not able to survive. Real life issues that created a need for her to have an encounter with a High Power and her coming out an overcomer.

Having five husbands within itself can be an issue. Why did she have five husbands? Nine times out of ten, back in that day, they all had passed away. That within itself would cause someone some major issues – grief, depression, stress and possible emotional instabilities.

The way my mind operates, I was given an entirely different revelation. One for a more modern time such as today. Her having five husbands could have been a lot deeper than just death. Yes, one could have passed away. Not that the manner of death should create any lesser pain. What if one died of natural causes, while another died at the hands of another human being. Some heinous, senseless act of the ever so poplar gun violence that plagues are streets. What if one was an abuser – emotional, verbal and physical? One could have had issues with infidelity, an addiction to drugs and alcohol, or problems repeating various offenses, causing him to go back and forth to prison.

These are situations that women go through in today's society. Situations that cause some of the issues we deal with on an everyday basis – lack of/low self-esteem, depression, anxiety, stress, emotional, physical and possibly sexual abuse, alcohol/substance abuse, grief, loss, unforgiving, pain, hurt, disappointment, rejection, grief/loss, health issues, and marriage/relationship issues.

Even though her pot was empty, this woman came to the well carrying a load. However, after her encounter with a Higher Power, she was filled. Now she was "Well". The very ones she used to hide from, she went running to. She ran to the women that constantly talked about her and put her down; to the men that used her and abused her; to those that lied on her and scandalized her name. She ran to share her encounter. To empower those that were in her community and to share the encounter she had with her High Power.

She came one way but did not leave the same. She came and was identified as the woman at the well, but she left a WELL Woman!!! So as we too go through our daily lives living with the issues of life, I have accepted a charge to help my fellow women, transition from being women at the well to becoming WELL Women!

MY JOURNEY

How Did I Get Here?

I have been broken pretty much all of my life. I grew up with very low self-esteem. It started at a very early age due to visible scarring I had no control over. Unlike most people I know that can tell you vivid memories of their childhood – their first day of kindergarten; who their best friend was in the 3rd grade; family vacations or home videos. My childhood memories take me back to the time a family friend was supposed to be babysitting, so I hid under the bed to keep from being violated; or me trying to remember the most amount of Barbie dolls I had collected, before having to leave them behind and start all over as we moved to another house; or why I had never completed a whole school year at the same school until the 7th grade.

I grew up in a somewhat dysfunctional home. Although it seemed the norm at the time – alcohol, family gatherings, card games and domestic violence situations, I thought that's just what families do. I have been violated by various family members and friends; raped at gun point (at the age of fourteen), and became a mother three months before turning sixteen (not associated with the rape). After several failed relationships, I found myself crying out, "Lord what is wrong with me!" I came to realize the type of men I was attracting was not good – cheaters, alcoholics, drug addicts and ex-cons. That just solidified my assumption that I was the one with the problem.

Not until late in my life did I recognize some other issues that plagued me for years. To add coal to the fire, per se, as an adult I have been homeless, incarcerated, lied on, cheated on, and emotionally abused. I was a poster child for mental health with depression, anxiety, isolation, bitterness, anger, fear, chronic stress and a whole lot of other issues and strongholds. I lived a life of negativism. I was just down right over it all. I could not win for losing. If it was not for bad luck, I did not seem to have any luck. Or so I thought.

How do you go through your whole life asking, "why me"? But then three quarters of the way through you realize, it had to be me! You come to the realization that everything you have gone through in your life was not just for you. It was for you to be a mouthpiece for others that may have to go through the same things. It was to empower someone else that may not be able to see their way out; for someone who believes there is no coming back from a past mistake; for that one that says I give up, I cannot do this any longer and contemplates taking their life, to end the hurt and pain. You constantly try to figure out, how did I get here and how do I get out? But not until you are able to accept where you are and why you are there, will you be able to move.

I would have never thought the things that I went through in my life would have been allowed by God. I always believed in God because I was told to and it just seemed like the right thing to do. But then one day it happened. I realized that there was an opportunity to help someone else. Through everything that I had gone through, it is like the sunshine mixed with rain to create a rainbow. I had my well experience. I had an encounter with a Power higher than I. I could look back on everything that happened in my life and see my purpose. I could see the purpose for the need to transition from being a woman at the well to being a "WELL Woman". I had to experience, "My Journey to the Well!"

The Pieces of Me –The Spiritual, Mental, Physical and Emotional

Despite not being able to fully remember some of the bad things from my childhood, I do remember some good things. I can tell you that family was everything. We had a large family and family gathers occurred daily, just because. There was never a time I don't remember a group of family members being together. I enjoyed the family meals and card games. I used to joke and say the first words that the kids in our family say are pity pat and tunk out; or 50 cents on spades -not the traditional momma or dada. They learn to play cards before they were potty trained. We may have fought each other like cats and dogs, but let an outsider mess with one of us. It was a wrap. I saw the love by everyone's presence.

I loved my family and all of our get-togethers. So why was I always so mad? Why was I always walking around frowning? I was constantly asked, why do you always look so mean? You look like you mad at the world. In essence, I was. Even though I had suppressed the memory of most of the bad things that had happened to me, deep down seeds had been planted- seeds of bitterness and resentment. And each time something bad happened, it resulted in those seeds being watered. Until finally they grew and manifested into bitterness and anger.

Anger is defined as a strong feeling of annoyance, displeasure or hostility. This began to be a constant feeling for me. Even though I did not smoke or drink, I loved being around my family. While everyone else was laughing and joking around, my inner man was eye balling them, like really? Outside of the permanent frown I wore, my outward appearance was fine. It was my inner man that was being choked out by all the dead weeds that were growing from the unhealthy seeds that had been planted. I think my inner man or inner woman, was annoyed at the fact that nobody could see me hurting inside. Everybody was quick to acknowledge the frown or the mean mug as they call it, but no one knew why. When they did ask, it was rhetorical. What was even more hurtful was the fact that I beat my own self up for not telling.

So now the seed of guilt is being watered. I am going back and forth within myself. If you would not have gone outside when you were told to stay in, you would never have gotten raped; if you had not have asked that family member for money to get into the card game, they would have never felt like they could touch you that way. Ok, well none of these things were my fault. So why didn't you tell? Silence. Nothing. I went mute on myself.

This is just one of the strategies the enemy used to keep my mind in bondage and created a phobia – a fear of speaking out loud or verbalizing myself in any capacity. I was so used to speaking in my mind, when it was time to speak out loud, I would freeze. This has caused me to fail in many areas of my life. In sixth grade, I had to do a report on

Zaire. I completed the report – grade A material. But because I did not present it orally, I received an F. I have gone through an entire semester of college courses and dropped out during the last week or choose to accept the failing grade, because I choose not to do the oral presentation. This is the story of my life. Over the years I had learned to internalize everything and just keep it to myself.

Along with bitterness, anger, guilt and fear, I also isolated myself internally. It became external in my later years. I would have full blown conversations in my head, with myself. Don't laugh, but I still do. But now the conversations are different. They are not all negative. I used to say I made up my dreams that way. I was fascinated when the movie *"Inside Out"* came out. I was like, "YES! I am normal! Somebody finally gets me!" Somebody actually gave a voice to the poplar emotions we deal with daily – joy, sadness, anger, fear and disgust. So my feelings were justified. I have experienced a real life battlefield of the mind.

So I learned to live with my insane state of mind, which did not help my emotional state.

To complicate my life even more, low self-esteem plagued me to the point that I accepted any attention that was pointed in my direction. I found myself "dating" unlikely individuals. I told myself it was because I felt sorry for them. But in reality, they showed me attention and I accepted it. I guess I was really the unlikely one. This topic along could be a book by itself, but I will settle for writing about it in my next book.

"Love is patient, love is kind. It does not envy, it does not boast, it is not proud. It does not dishonor others, it is not self-seeking, it is not easily angered, it keeps no record of wrongs. Love does not delight in evil but rejoices with the truth. It always protects, always trusts, always hopes, always perseveres."
I Corinthians 13: 1-7

You cannot show love if it is not in you.

What's Love Got To Do With It?

What's love got to do with it? Is that just another catchy cliché or does it really have a meaning. A lot of people confuse loving someone with being in love. What is love? As with most other words love has a number of meanings and can be used in various forms such as a noun and a verb. Love is defined as an intense feeling of deep affection, a person or thing that one loves or to feel a deep romantic or sexual attraction to someone. In the Greek there are eight different types of love, four of which are the most common. Eros or Phila which is erotic or affectionate love - the love you would feel for a spouse or significant other. Storge or a familiar love – as for your children or other family members. And the best love of all being Agape love, which is selfless love or the love of Christ.

How is it that someone can say they love you, but yet can tell you anything and everything but the truth. They imply certain things about you (referring to you as a whore or hoe), but claim they are joking. I was told that there is a lot of truth in a joke. You get called all kinds of derogatory names. They lie and manipulate their way through the relationship. You would have done anything to keep them happy, but the more you do, the more they take advantage of the relationship. Manipulators never question themselves. They don't see themselves as the problem. The problem is always someone else.

A lot of people confuse loving someone, with being in love. If an individual (male or female), is treating you any kind of way – lying, cheating, stealing, and disrespecting you, you don't have to stay with them because you love them. But do they love you? They tell you that they do, but if they loved you like they say they do, they would not treat you the way they do. Words lie, actions don't.

You do not have to accept anyone's constant disrespect and manipulation. That is not love. He/she hits you or displays verbal and emotional abuse; that is not love. Why do you stay? Because you have children; because you are married? Never accept anything less than what you deserve. You should not have to rip yourself to pieces to keep others whole. You teach people how to treat you, by what you allow. Remember, if it costs you your peace, than it is too expensive.

You do not have to settle. No matter how much time you have invested in a person. There is always someone out there that will love you like you deserve to be loved. But the solution is not waiting on the next one to fix what the last one broke. The solution is to allow God to heal you and help you regain your self- worth, so when that right person finds you, they can just add to what is already there.

I used to joke about an immaculate conception taking place with my oldest three children. When someone would ask me about birthing them, I used to say God had three little people that needed to be taken care of and He thought I was the best one to do the job. So can you imagine the thoughts that ran through my mind when I began to feel better about my life and start loving myself, only to get the feeling that I did not love my children? These three little people that did not ask to come in to this world; these three little people that assisted me into my transition from being a girl, to being a woman so much sooner than the time I had planned.

How can you be a mother and not love your own children. That devastated me to no end. I pressed my way after dropping out of high school twice, to get my GED. I even went a step further to get my high school diploma, to show them that education matters. And that anything is obtainable no matter what situation you may find yourself in. But in my mind, I did not love them. I busted my behind working, from the age of fourteen and worked even harder after each one of them were born. Sometimes working two jobs at a time to provide the necessities required by law and human nature. But in my mind, I did not love them. I did everything within my power to protect them from the issues and cares of this world; to shield them from the evil that presented itself on a daily basis in the streets. I tried to protect them from the heartaches and the love woes of settling for less than you deserve for the sake of love. But in my mind I did not love them. Or so I thought.

I had a meltdown because in my mind I could not possibly love my children because I did not verbally tell them that I loved them. This was another result of those seeds that were planted in my earlier life, growing into weeds trying to choke out my life. I had learned to be mute to everything.

I could not recall speaking the actual words I Love You, out of my mouth to my children. I see people do it on a regular basis. I have family members that do it faithfully. But that was not my story. Why was that? Was it because I could not recall having it said to me on a regular basis by my parents? They showed. As long as I showed it, that should have been enough, right? Was it because we never really formed that mother to child bond due to being incarcerated when they were younger. I had only been gone for ten months and the last five and a half I was coming home on the weekends. Although, they were still only four, two and the baby had just turned one, two weeks prior.

Was it because I talked at them instead of talking to them? It was more like yelling most times. Not realizing I was projecting the anger and bitterness of my life at them. There was some stress associated with being a single teenage mother, two times over. But I thank and praise God for supplying the help that I needed. I found myself sitting down with my spiritual mother crying out in despair. She helped me get a grip on my life and reassured me that my actions spoke the love I had for my children, and she helped me learn how to use my words.

God sent me to a church with a loving Pastor and First Lady. A church that seemed to have been built on LOVE! It was a Sunday in October of 1996. I had just had an abortion the Friday before. That day I learned to never say what I would never do. My oldest was six and my youngest was two. I had only been out of prison completely for about eight months and was still trying to build a relationship with them. I visited the church at the persistence of a friend asking me to go. However, after going a few more times here and there, I joined a year later. Not only was it the Word – I was able to understand it a little clearer now. But it was the love of the people. They greeted you with love when you walked in and treated you as if you were a member from the day the doors opened. There were no big I's and no little U's. They did not want to hear your story to be nosey and gossip, but they prayed and showed genuine compassion and concern for not only your soul, but also for you well-being.

The bible says that the power of life and death are in our tongue. And we are taught to speak those things that are not as though they are. It was through this show of love that I began to re-evaluate my life and the love I had for my children.

THE WELL

Your greatest ministry will most likely come out of your greatest hurt.

In order for us to be effective in ministry, we must first be affected by the ministry. The biblical story of the Woman at the Well, in John chapter 4, is a part of the ministry God gave me. The woman at the well came with various issues. We too come with a variety of issues. They may not all be the same, but at the end of the day they are all issues. As I stated previously, I struggled with a whole lot of issues. Issues that had my life falling apart. I had to learn that sometimes when things are falling apart, they may actually be falling into place. I had to go through these things to fulfill my purpose. My purpose being to change in a way that I can draw and lead others out (to the well).

It is at the well where our transition takes place. We sit and talk with Jesus (prayer); we begin to lose our issues one by one. As we get rid of our issues, we begin to transition from being the woman at the well to being a well woman. To understand this concept I will take you through a few short stories about how I had to be afflicted (affected) in order to be effective.

Home Sweet Home

Homelessness is not a disease. It is not something most people chose. It is however a condition of people without a permanent dwelling. People who are homeless are most often unable to acquire and maintain regular, safe, secure and adequate housing. Nowadays when we see or hear about homeless people, the first thing that comes to our mind is those that are plagued with drug and alcohol issues. Our mind does is go to what is known as skid row; to the individuals that we pass by down under the bridge next to the Sunday Breakfast Mission or the ones that hang out drinking in Christiana Park by day, and sleeping under the pavilion at night; to the ones that do not have and most likely cannot keep a job; the ones you see standing in the lines at the dining hall waiting for breakfast and lunch to be serve and trying to make it back to the other places in time for dinner. Those are the ones we think about when we hear someone talking about the homeless. Well that was not my story and I have been homeless on quite a few occasions.

I had worked most of my life, with the exception of a few months here and there from being in between assignments with the temporary agencies or out due to being in a car accident. This particular time I had been in my third car accident within a five year stretch. I had gotten backed up in my rent for the second time and the property manager said they had done all they could do. The owner wanted their property back.

What was I going to do, where was I going to go? I was a single mother with three children at this time. All of the shelters were full and not taking any new families. I had a church sister I was able to go stay with on a temporary basis. However, that was not an issue. The issue was I was embarrassed. How is it that all my life I have taken care of other people's children, given others a place to stay and now I cannot provide shelter for my own children. How can I call myself a mother and look my children in the face, as we lay down to sleep in someone's basement. I had failed as a mother. So now, the seed of guilt and shame gets watered and begins to grow again. After staying in the friend's basement for a short period, a room opened at one of the emergency family shelters. We shared living quarters with other families in similar situations. Some had job, some did not. We had to share the daily chores such as cooking and cleaning and being able to co-habitat with people of different cultures and backgrounds. After out thirty day stay, with a ten day extension, we transitioned into another emergency facility that became available. After a brief ten day stay, God opened up an opportunity at a transitional housing facility that generally only accepted women who were being released from prison or a drug and alcohol facility. Nether was the case with me. But God.

This facility was similar to the others, but there were a few more stipulations. We had to work and pay bills. This time we not only had to clean and cook, but we were also responsible for creating a weekly meal plan and a shopping list to go with it. We also had to actually go shopping for the food and stick to the budget we were instructed to create. Along with budgeting our money for bills and food, we had to save. We had to create a plan of action to assist our future transition.

There was another instance of homelessness for us. By this time, I had been approved for a Section 8 voucher for housing and had been in the program for a few years and had been doing great. I went through a period of working part time, along with not working at all. But at this time I had a full time job and was everything seemed to be going well. It was going so well I had decided to upgrade and move. Transitioning from a 3 bedroom in the heart of the city to a 4 bedroom, one and a half bath, and a full basement, in the county. After finding a place and doing every that needed to be done my exit date came. I was all ready to move out, however my new place was not ready for me to move in.

By now my previous three children were teenagers, but now I have a two year old and a newborn. Wow! Another blow to the head. My mental state that is. Here I am with a full time job, with benefits. Not that that matters, but I am now homeless – AGAIN! It just so happened I was working at Welfare to Work program that also housed an emergency shelter. I am not sure if it was the fear of being told no; they stayed full. Did I mention I had a fear of rejection? Maybe it was pride – I didn't want those people all in my busy. There was this one social worker who knew everyone in Wilmington; I didn't want her going around telling my business. Not to mention we had clients that stayed there as well. Whatever it was I decided to put it aside and ask for help. I was told to come in after work Wow! Low and behold. God did it again.

I stayed in the shelter for about two weeks. It was a holiday week so it was not two full weeks. But the idea of having to be in at a certain time, in order to keep your bed; having to wake up and be out of the building at a certain time. That really was not an issue, since I had to take the boys to daycare so I could get back to work. But can you imagine, waking up in a place where you share a community wash room with individuals that you see in your work place in a different capacity? Or having the child care workers that know you work in the building, see you walking through the laundry area to get to that same community bathroom to wash. If that does not humble a person and cause the death of pride, I do not know what will. Until this day, I thank and praise God for those times. I thank him for the lessons that were learned from each experience and for the testimony I can give to empower other women that may find themselves in similar situations.

Disconnect Notice

Have you ever fallen behind in payment of maybe your electric bill? If you do not pay the bill within a certain time frame, the electric company will send you a disconnect notice. This notice reminds you that your bill is past due. It tells you that you have until a certain day to pay a certain amount or else they will disconnect your electric services.

I read that the word disconnect means to sever the connection of or between, to dissociate, to terminate a connection or to become detached. Have you ever had to dissociate or sever a connection with someone? How did it feel? What about having someone terminate a connection with you? How did that make you feel?

I have had relationships (using the word interchangeable with friendships) come and go. Some were good and some were bad. It did not matter if it was a good one or a bad one, the "disconnect" was never easy. It was evident that some of these losses needed to take place, no matter who or what the cause was. Especially the ones that only call you when they need something or just to gossip. Then there were the ones that call you crying over something and you were there to listen and console them with words of encouragement, but when you call them to cry or vent, you had to snap out of it and get over it. Let's not leave out the ones that somehow always managed to turn the conversation into being about them.

The worst type of disconnection is the ones that occur and you had no idea it was taking place. Everything seemed good. Just like it always been. One day you realize that you haven't heard from them because you hadn't had the time or energy to reach out. That's when it hit you. You were the one always initiating the phone calls and the texts, unless they needed or wanted something. You realized they never sacrificed; it was always a convenience for them. Wow! That hurts.

Stop going out of your way for people who only view you as a convenience and letting people who do so little for you control so much of your mind, feelings and emotions. You are allowed to terminate toxic relationships; you are allowed to walk away from people who hurt you. You do not owe anyone an explanation for taking care of you.

The disconnections in your life can be good or bad, but they always serve a purpose. Some of them are strategies of the enemy to keep your mind in bondage. After losing my First Lady, I had a hard time focusing. I left the door open for the enemy to set up camp in my mind. Apparently, I was not the only one. I got accused of sleeping with my pastor. This man was like a father to me. He raised me up from a babe in Christ to the awesome anointing woman of God I am today.

It was very difficult to sit week after week in the face of someone who started such a vicious lie. My attendance at the church declined. When you lose your passion for going to church; to lose the fear of God - that is a dangerous place to be in. I went back into the world. It was really cunning the way it all happened. In my mind I was consoling a family member get through the death of a loved one and I called myself meeting her where she was at. However, because I was losing the joy of the Lord, I was not strong enough to resist the temptations. My heart was always with the Lord, however my physical body went back to what I knew best- fornicating and hanging out with people that showed me attention. And the music. Music was always a comforter to me, whether I was in the church or out of it. So to find myself hanging in the clubs was not a surprise. I was not a real drinker – Boones Farm or a Jack Daniels wine cooler would have me grooving, But I was in my element; being swayed by the music and dancing all night.

I won't bore you with all the details (a story for another time); however, I had a prodigal child moment and found my way back to the house of

God. It was during this transition that the Lord gave me the analogy of the disconnection. It seemed as if I was not connected to the true source of power - Jesus. I was connected by way of an extension cord or generator in the form of my First Lady and a few others. Once this was brought to my attention, like the prodigal son, I came to my senses and came back home – to the church.

You would think after being away off and on for three years and being engaged, all the hoopla would have ceased. Not so. I guess I was not the only one that had some seeds planted in an earlier life, that that needed to be uprooted.

Sometimes God will put a Goliath in your path for you to discover the in you. David did not know the strength of Goliath; neither did he care, because he knew the strength of the God that was within himself. Sometimes you don't know your own strength until somebody tries to take advantage of your weaknesses.

It was very difficult, however I confronted that devil head on – NOT THIS TIME DEVIL!!! I was determined not to allow the enemy to win. He was not going to run me away this time. When I got unfairly attacked, the enemy did not realize God would turn it into a God given unfair advantage. It was a struggle to get back to where I should have been in the Lord. It is still a constant race. But I find comfort in knowing that it is not how fast or slow you go, but that you endure until the end.

Walking in Wellness

What is a well? We are taught about the different parts of speech and their meanings in grade school. The word well can be defined a number of ways. It can be defined as an adverb, an adjective, an exclamation, a noun or a verb.

As an adverb it could mean -in a good or satisfactory way; in a way that is appropriate to the facts or circumstances; so as to have a fortunate outcome; in a kind way or with praise or approval. As an adverb it could also mean in a thorough manner, in a condition of prosperity or comfort, or without difficulty.

As an adjective the word is used to define one in good health, free or recovered from illness or someone in a satisfactory state or position.

A noun is defined as a word used to name a person, place, thing or idea. With that being said the word well as define as a noun could be a plentiful source or supply, a region of minimum potential, or a shaft sunk into the ground to obtain water, oil or gas.

When I think about my journey to the well, look at the various forms of the word being used. I guess I would consider myself as: a woman dealing with the issues of life, going to a plentiful source or supply; to obtain water (living water) or oil (the anointing); but leaving in a condition of prosperity or comfort, in good health, free or recovered from illness.

The fourth chapter of the Book of John tells us the story of the Samaritan Woman or The Woman at the Well. It tells us that Jesus had a need to go through the city of Samaria on his way to Galilee. For Jesus to have a need to go out of his way there had to be a problem that needed his attention. As he gets to the town of Sychar he stops at Jacobs' well.

Like Queen Ester, the Woman at the well was predestined to be at the right place at the right time to deliver her people. They were both responsible for a village of people getting saved and delivered out of the hands of the enemy.

I appreciate the things that molded me into a better woman. Even when it hurt or I did not understand. It was needed for who I have become. When I look in the mirror after all the hurts and scars. God had a purpose for the pain. I can say I made it. I survived that which was supposed to take me out. God never promised that it would be easy, but He did promise to be me through it all.

From a Woman at the Well to a WELL Woman

After all that I have gone through, sometimes I had to stop and look back to see how I made it. How can I now part my lips to say IT IS WELL or that I AM WELL! It was not always easy. Anytime you are trying to do right and do what the Lord called you to do. The enemy will always bring distractions. Some days I wanted to throw in the towel. I told myself, what's the use? You might as well quit.

It was because of my negative mindset that I would always want to give up, but I had to remind myself as a great Woman of God used to tell me - The good news is the bad news is wrong. The Lord also sends me reminders that it is well and that this too shall pass!

Some of the issues women (and men) deal with on an everyday basis include: lack of/low self-esteem, depression, anxiety, stress, emotional, physical and possibly sexual abuse, alcohol/substance abuse, grief, loss, unforgiving, pain, hurt, disappointment, rejection, grief/loss, health issues, and marriage/relationship issues. These issues are real and will cause extreme interruptions in one's everyday life. Once you have had your well experience, I am not saying everything will be a bed of rose. You will still have to work to maintain your wellness. Here are a few things I do to maintain my wellness.

- **I pray!**
    - Prayer is a solemn request for help or expression of thanks addressed to God or an object of worship; an earnest hope or wish. Prayer works. It changes things. I know it sounds very clique, but it is the truth. I know it works, because it works for me.

All through the bible we are given examples of individuals that prayed when things got rough. For instance, David. With all that he did in his life; the good and the bad. He prayed. God heard him and He answered him. With losing all he had, including his children, Job prayed. God restored him. The bible tells us that even Jesus prayed. If Jesus did it, why shouldn't we? The Woman at the Well prayed. Her prayer was not recorded as the other prayers. Her prayer was in the form of a general conversation with Jesus. She was able to talk directly to the source, and He answered her. She came to draw earthly water, but instead was blessed with living water.

- **I journal!**
  - Journaling helps get your feelings out. I am the type of person that does not express myself well. I would bottle all of my feelings and emotions up on the inside. I learned from

experience that is not good. You can only fit but so much into any container. After a while if you continue filling up that same container without releasing anything out of it, it will eventually explode. I was not one to do well with verbalizing my feelings, but after a few explosive episodes, I learned that I can write my feelings out.

There are a few ways you can do this. You can write it out, ball it up and throw it away. You can also write it out in a journal. This way you can keep it and refer back to it when you have reached your goals and or accomplishments. You can look back to see your growth and how far you have come to overcome your issue. *(I've added some writing space in the back of the book for you to start journaling!)*

- **I connect!**
  - o Surround yourself with positive/like-minded people.

This was a big one for me. I realized that I was constantly surrounded by negative people or people who did not have the same goals or mindset as me. Negative people can bring a person's spirit down and they won't even realize it. They will slowly begin to look at everything from a negative prospective. They will have you murmuring and complaining. You will begin to realize you are going around in circles and not even realizing it. You will become like the children of Israel walking in the wilderness for 40 days, when it should have only been an 11 day journey. Be sure to evaluate your surroundings – people, places and things, on a regular basis.

- **I seek help!**
  - o Therapy and counseling is also another option. Although you don't see many in the African American or

the Religious community going this route. It is the stigma attached to being labeled for having issues But I am a firm believer that is why most, if not all, of us are in the situations we are in because of generation curses and the motto – what goes on in this house, stays in this house.

When you are being molested by family members but can't tell anybody for fear of what the neighbors will think. "Well Uncle Peewee has been doing this to girls in the family for years," but we are not supposed to talk about it. You allow the young girls to walk around half dressed, because that is what they see in the movies and latest music videos.

One day they are innocent young girls, the next day they are, having sex, by day three they are gay or bi-sexual, because that is the latest fad. Before you know it up they are having babies.

They follow suit with the same skimpy outfits and allow them to watch the same provocative music videos and foolish reality TV shows; and they think it's cute. Got a 4 year old gyrating to the latest rap songs and you wonder why every time Uncle Johnny come around he always got her bouncing on his knee. You should be teaching her how to say her ABCs, instead of celebrating the fact that she knows the words to Beyoncé's new CD.

- **I settle my spirit!**
  - Speaking of music... Music is another form of helping and healing. Whatever mood I am in, there is always a song or a playlist I can turn to assist me in my wellness journey. With that, I will also say that you must be careful of what you listen to.

I don't suggest you listen to R. Kelly, bumping and grinding or Silk asking to lick you up and down, if you are trying to abstain from fornicating. It is easy to fall into an even deeper slump if you are listening to Mary J. Blige after a break up. It is ok to listen, but don't wallow in it. It will hurt you more than help you by causing bitterness and anger to set in. Instead I recommend something inspirational. Something to uplift your spirit rather than bring it down even more or getting you all worked up and excited.

These are just a few ways that you can be empowered to walk in wellness. There are other things you can do like meditation, walking, exercise and yoga or reading books. I recommend including the bible when making your selection.

I have included a few local resources to assist you in your journey to wellness. I pray that you find comfort in these wellness tools.

WELL WOMAN EMPOWERMENT

When you replace "I" with "we", even illness becomes wellness!

Resources

Well Woman Empowerment Association
302 643-9885
PO Box 30771, Wilmington, DE 19805
Description: A support group for women which promotes spiritual, mental, physical, emotional and financial wellness.

National Alliance on Mental Health in Delaware
(NAMI DE)
302 427-0787
2400 W. 4th Street, Wilmington, DE 19805
Description: NAMI DE is a statewide organization of families, mental health consumers, friends, and professionals dedicated to improving the quality of life for those affected by life changing disorders.

DE Coalition Against Domestic Violence
302 658-2958
100 W. 10th Street, St#903, Wilmington, DE 19801
Description: DCADV is the statewide, nonprofit coalition of agencies and individuals working to stop domestic violence in Delaware

Mental Health Association of DE
302 654-6833
100W. 10th Street, St#600, Wilmington, DE 19801
Description: The Mental Health Association in Delaware promotes improved mental well-being for all individuals and families in Delaware through education, support, and advocacy.

Child Inc.
302 762-8989
507 Philadelphia Pike, Wilmington, DE 19809
Description: To provide creative prevention and treatment programs that meet the changing needs of families

Survivors of Abuse in Recovery (S.O.A.R)
405 Foulk Road, Wilmington, DE 19803
302 655-3953
Description: A non-profit organization dedicated to providing professional mental health services to victims of sexual trauma and their families.

Alcohol Anonymous
302 655-511
21B Trolley Square, Wilmington, DE 19806
Description: An alcoholism treatment program

About the Author

Keyshia Anderson was born and raised in Wilmington, DE. She is married, has six children and 8 grandchildren. She holds an Associates in General Studies from Wilmington, University and a Bachelors in Biblical Studies from the Enlightened Bible Institute. She is also waiting in enroll to get certified in Christian Counseling. She has worked in the Human Service field for nine years.

Keyshia is very big on education. She believes it is a necessity to succeed in life. She currently works with adults to obtain their GED and is the founder of Well Woman Empowerment Association.

Well Woman Empowerment Association was launched in January 2015. It is a network of women from all walks of life, that decided to join forces to not only empower themselves, but other women also, to be Well – spiritually, mentally, physically and emotionally. It is a faith based group, but it is not focused on any one religion.

Women are empowered to connect with their Higher Power to help overcome their issues and strongholds, as the Samaritan Women did when she had an encounter with Jesus at the well.

A PORTION OF EVERY BOOK SOLD
WILL BE DONATED TO THE WELL
WOMAN EMPOWERMENT
ASSOCIATION

Pieces of Me by Ledisi

People just don't know what I'm about, they haven't seen what's there behind my smile, There's so much more of me I'm showing now, These are the pieces of me, When it looks like I'm up sometimes I'm down, I'm lonely even when people all around, but that don't change the happiness I've found. These are the pieces of me

You see when you look at my face, you gotta know that I'm made of everything love and pain, these are the pieces of me, Like every woman I know, I'm complicated to show, But when I love I love until there's no love no more, these are the pieces of me, So many colors, Make up this woman that you see, A good friend and lover, anything you want yes I can be, I can run the business and make time for fantasy, these are the pieces of me. Now I'm gonna make mistakes from time to time, But in the end believe it I'm gonna fly, No matter if I'm wrong or if I'm right, these are the pieces of me, Ohhh as the pieces of me start to unfold, now I start to understand, all that I am, A woman not afraid to be strong, So when you look at my face you gotta know that I'm made of everything love and pain, These are the pieces of me, Like every woman I know I'm complicated to show but when I love I love til there's no more, these are the pieces of me, I'm a woman...a woman... a woman woman-woman

Yes I'm a woman... a woman... these are the pieces of me.

WELL WOMAN JOURNALING

_____

_____

_____

_____

_____

_____

_____

_____

_____

_____

_____

_____

_____